WALT DISNEY
STORY BOOKS

WALT DISNEY STORY BOOKS

DONALD DUCK AND
HIS FRIENDS

Told by

JEAN AYER

Illustrated by

THE WALT DISNEY STUDIO

D. C. HEATH AND COMPANY

BOSTON

STORIES IN THE BOOK

DONALD'S OSTRICH

Mickey Mouse and Donald Duck went to the railway station. They went to wave good-by to Minnie Mouse. Minnie was going to the city to get a new dress.

After the train had gone, they walked along the station platform. There they saw — what do you think — an ostrich!

1

The ostrich was rather pretty. There was a big card on a ribbon around her neck. The card said,

"Hortense Ostrich. In care of Henry P. Ostrich, Green Tree Hill."

"There won't be a train to Green Tree Hill for two hours," said Mickey. "She'll have to wait."

Donald said, "Hello, Hortense." The ostrich didn't say anything.

"The cat's got her tongue," said Donald.

"Look, Donald," said Mickey. "The other side of Hortense's card says, 'Do not annoy.'"

"Well, I'm not going to annoy her," said Donald. "Are you?"

"Certainly not," said Mickey.

"Probably she's hungry," said Donald. "Perhaps that's why she acts so d-u-m-b. We ought to get her something to eat. What do ostriches eat, Mickey?"

"I don't know," said Mickey. "I'll run home and get my book about birds. That will tell us what to feed her."

While Mickey was gone, Donald tried to talk to Hortense. But Hortense would not say a word.

"It's too bad you won't talk," said Donald. "We could play a game and have some fun."

Hortense didn't say anything in reply to this, either. But she looked very pleasant. She was looking at Donald's cap.

3

"Do you like my new cap?" asked Donald. "It's just like the baggage master's cap. I got it to wear when I play I am working on the railroad."

Just then Mickey came back in a great hurry. He was carrying the book about birds.

Donald and Mickey sat down near Hortense on a little green trunk. They began to read the book.

"See. It says birds should eat bird-seed," said Mickey.

"It says to give them fruit, too," said Donald. "I don't think bird-seed would be enough for an ostrich. Hortense is no canary."

"I have some money," said Mickey. "So I'll go to the store and get some bird-seed. We can give her a whole box of it. That ought to make her feel better."

"I'll go home," said Donald, "and see what I can find there."

In a short time they were back again. Mickey had a box of bird-seed. Donald carried a lunch box. He opened the box and showed a big piece of cake, a sandwich, a banana, and a tomato. They looked very good.

They opened the box of bird-seed and offered that to Hortense first.

She turned her head away and acted as if she did not know it was good to eat.

"Try the cake," said Mickey.

So Donald offered Hortense the big, beautiful piece of cake. Hortense sniffed at the cake, but she would not touch it.

They tried the tomato. She did not want that, either.

Donald brought out next the sandwich and the banana. Hortense didn't want these. She didn't seem interested at all.

Donald began to be angry. He thought Hortense was just trying to be disagreeable. But she still looked pleasant. She kept her eyes on Donald's cap. It seemed to please her.

"I don't think you are very polite to us, Hortense," said Donald. "You might just *taste* what we brought you."

"Never mind, Donald," said Mickey. "We can eat your things ourselves."

But Donald went right on scolding.

7

"Mickey paid his own money for
that bird-seed, Hortense," he said,
"and I brought you a big, big piece of
cake — and you don't even say 'Thank
you.' You won't get anything to eat
on the train, and I hope you don't
get anything at Green Tree Hill,
either — you old feather duster!"

8

"Don't talk like that, Donald," said Mickey. "I don't believe Hortense means to be rude. Probably she just doesn't feel like eating."

"But I think she *looks* hungry," said Donald. "She keeps looking at me as if she were hungry."

Just then the baggage master came along. He was going to put Hortense on the train. He saw the food Mickey and Donald had brought.

"Hortense isn't hungry," he said. "She has had her dinner. She might like small stones or some nails or buttons or pieces of cloth. She likes to eat a few rough things after her dinner. All ostriches do."

"Why didn't she tell us?" asked Mickey.

9

"She grew up in Africa," said the baggage master. "She doesn't know much English."

"Well, if she sees anything she wants, she can help herself," said Donald. "I'm through trying to feed her."

At these words, Hortense reached down and picked off Donald's cap. Before they could stop her, she had swallowed it — visor, buttons, and all.

"Oh, oh, oh! My cap! My cap!" said Donald.

Hortense paid no attention to Donald's cries. She marched off to the train, still looking pleasant.

"Well, Donald," said Mickey, "you told her to help herself, and she did. So you can't complain."

THE NEW WAGON

Donald Duck was walking down the street pulling his new express wagon. He was very proud of the express wagon. It was painted green and red and looked quite gay.

When Donald came to Pluto's house, Pluto was in the front yard digging a hole.

"Hi, Pluto," said Donald, "come on along with me. I'll let you be my horse and pull my new wagon."

"I don't want to be a horse," said Pluto.

"Oh, come on," said Donald. "You can be an Eskimo dog, if you'd rather."

"All right," said Pluto. "I'll be an Eskimo dog."

Donald took the red leather collar and traces out of the wagon. He put the collar around Pluto's neck and fastened the traces to the wagon.

Then Donald sat down in the express wagon and shouted, "Mush!"

"What about it?" said Pluto.

"What about what?" said Donald.

"What about mush?" said Pluto.

"Oh," said Donald, "when an Eskimo wants his dogs to go, he says 'Mush.' "

"What does he say when he wants them to stop — Oatmeal?" asked Pluto.

"I don't know," said Donald. "But you won't have to stop till you get to Mr. Growler's house. He wants the things I have in this box for lunch. He'll pay me a dime for bringing them from the market. I have to do a great many things with my express wagon today. I want to cover a lot of ground. Mush, you old Eskimo dog!"

Pluto stepped off briskly. The wagon, even with its load, didn't seem very heavy. He enjoyed pulling it over the level ground. Playing that he was an Eskimo dog was fun.

Then Donald had an idea. It seemed like a very good idea to him.

"Say, Pluto," said Donald. "If you go up the hill to Mr. Growler's house, instead of going around, we'll save quite a lot of time."

But Pluto didn't like the idea.

"It's hard to pull uphill," said Pluto.

"Oh, go ahead, lazybones!" said Donald.

So Pluto started up the hill. It was
very steep. Pluto thought Donald
should get out and walk. But Donald
Duck sat still. Poor old Pluto put his
feet down hard and pulled the wagon
slowly forward.

"You'd better get out and walk,
Donald," said Pluto.

Pluto was pulling hard by now, for the hill grew steeper and steeper.

"I have to stay in the wagon," said Donald. "I have to see that the things for Mr. Growler's lunch don't fall out of the box."

By this time Pluto, who had been pulling very hard, was nearly at the top of the hill.

Suddenly there came a snap. Then there was another snap. Pluto felt his load grow very light, and Donald shouted in alarm.

The traces were not very strong They had broken — first one and then the other.

The express wagon flew backward down the hill while Donald hung on for dear life.

16

The things Mr. Growler had ordered
went flying out along the way — some
cans of soup, a box of sardines, a bottle
of catsup. A string of frankfurters
flew out like a flag of danger. But
they were not lost because Donald was
standing on one end of the string.

17

Near the foot of the hill the express wagon struck a rock. It bounced into the air and came down in pieces, with Donald on top of the pieces.

At first, after the traces broke, Pluto had felt like laughing because Donald looked so funny flying down the hill. But now he hurried after Donald to help him.

"Oh, Donald, are you hurt?" he cried.

"Not much," said Donald. He stood up with the string of frankfurters hanging around his neck. "But look at my wagon — all in pieces! You should have been more careful, Pluto. You pulled too hard on those traces. If you hadn't pulled so hard they wouldn't have broken."

Pluto thought this was not fair, but he was too kind to say so. He began brushing dirt off Donald.

"Anyhow, Donald," he said, "you wanted to cover a lot of ground, and you certainly *have* covered a lot of ground. Let's pick up the pieces of your wagon. Perhaps Mickey can put them together again. He's very good at fixing things."

"We'd better pick up Mr. Growler's things, too," said Donald. "I need that dime."

Mickey really did fix the wagon. And Mr. Growler got the things he had ordered. He didn't know how much traveling they had done, for Donald and Pluto didn't tell him.

DONALD'S DOG SHOW

"I've been to the dog show," said Mickey one day to Donald and Pluto.

"What did you see?" asked Donald.

"I saw a great many dogs," said Mickey. "There were judges to pick out the best dogs. The dog that got the first prize was a poodle."

"My goodness!" said Pluto, "why did they want to give a prize to a poodle? I think poodles are silly-looking things."

21

"You ought to have seen this poodle," said Mickey. "He was all fixed up. He was one of the long-haired kind, but his hair had been clipped off. That is, it had almost all been clipped off. They had left enough for cuffs around his front legs, and another cuff around his tail."

"That pup must have looked like a regular sissy," said Donald.

"They say," said Pluto, "that the dogs that are in a show all have to be washed first with a lot of soap."

"That poodle dog had been washed, all right," said Mickey. "He was as clean as silk. The lady who owned him even sprayed some scent on him so that he would smell nice. I saw her do it."

"I should think it would have made him sick," said Pluto.

"Say," said Donald suddenly, "why don't we have a dog show? We can tell everyone who has a dog to bring it and put it in the show. We can have the show this afternoon. Mr. Growler has gone to the city. We can have the show in his garage."

"What can we have for prizes?" asked Mickey.

"We can charge everyone who comes to the show five cents," said Donald. "Then we can give two prizes out of the money we take in. We can keep most of the money. The prizes at dog shows are just pieces of ribbon. Anyhow, our dog will probably take the first prize."

23

"We haven't any dog to put in a show," said Mickey.

"We have Pluto," said Donald.

"I won't be in a show," said Pluto. "I'm not handsome enough."

"We can fix you up so that you'll look fine. If you'll be in the show," said Donald, "Mickey and I will divide the money with you."

"Will you, Mickey?" asked Pluto.

"Yes, we will, Pluto," said Mickey.

"All right," said Pluto. "Then I'll be in the show — but I don't think much of the idea."

24

"We'd better get Pluto ready now," said Donald. He was afraid Pluto would change his mind.

Mickey and Donald got a tub of warm water and a big cake of soap. Pluto stood in the tub and they gave him a good scrubbing. To help out, Donald got a hose and turned it on Pluto to wash off the soapsuds.

They dried Pluto with a bath towel. Then they had him sit on a box so that he wouldn't get dirty again.

"He looks very plain for a show dog," said Donald. "He ought to have a ruff and some cuffs like that dog you saw, Mickey.

"My mother has a little fur rug," Donald went on. "I don't think she cares much about it. It's pretty old. We can cut that up and make Pluto a ruff and some cuffs."

"They won't stay on," said Mickey.

"We can put them on with glue," said Donald.

"You'll have to take them off right after the show," said Pluto.

"Oh, we will," said Mickey.

Donald dashed off to get the rug, and Mickey went home for a pot of glue.

Pluto waited till they came back.

He wasn't very happy, but he didn't want to run away and disappoint Mickey and Donald.

They soon came back with the rug and the glue. They cut a strip from the rug and made a ruff for Pluto's neck. Then they made cuffs for his front legs and another cuff for his tail.

Then Donald sprayed Pluto to make him smell nice. He used an atomizer he had found at home. There was medicine in the atomizer. It had a very queer smell.

"Pluto, you look grand," said Donald. He tied a long red ribbon to Pluto's collar to lead him by.

"You do look nice, Pluto," said Mickey. "I'll get a mirror so you can see yourself."

Mickey hurried home and came
back with a mirror. He set the mirror
up in front of Pluto. Donald stood
proudly by, holding the red ribbon.

Pluto looked at himself. What he
saw looked very, very odd to him.
The medicine smelled worse and
worse. Suddenly he felt that, money
or no money, he didn't want to be
in Donald's dog show.

He gave a flying leap and ran away as hard as he could go.

Donald hung, shouting, to the red ribbon. But the ribbon broke, and Donald was soon left far behind.

He walked back to Mickey. "We can't have a show, now," he said. "I think Pluto was mean to run away. I'll tell him so when he comes back."

"He didn't want to be in the show," said Mickey; "and we knew he didn't. So we were mean, too. We won't see him again till he gets all that stuff off. I'm not going to say anything about the show when he comes back. You'd better let him alone, too."

"Oh, all right," said Donald. "Let's do something else. We can just forget about the dog show."

THE BOAT BUILDERS

Donald and Mickey and Goofy were down by the shore. They were sailing a toy boat. Some one had given it to Goofy.

By and by, the water got a little rough, and the toy boat tipped over. So Goofy took it out of the water.

The three friends sat on a rock.

"What shall we do now?" Donald wanted to know.

"Wouldn't it be fun if we had a boat of our own?" said Goofy. "I mean a boat big enough to sail in."

"We could make one," said Mickey. "We could make it like Goofy's little boat, only much larger. There are lots of boards lying around on the shore."

"Good!" said Donald. "I'll go and get a hammer and some nails."

"I'll get a saw and some glue," said Mickey.

"We could use a window shade for a sail," said Donald.

"I'll bring one," said Goofy. "My mother took an old shade down yesterday. She doesn't want it."

Donald and Mickey and Goofy worked hard over the boat. It took them three days to build it. They got some paint and painted the outside white with a red border. They painted the inside green.

Donald was afraid a high tide might carry the boat away. So he borrowed anchors from some of the people who lived along the shore.

One anchor would have held the boat very nicely. But Donald tied four anchors to it, just to be sure.

At last, the boat was all finished.

"Tomorrow morning," said Mickey, "we will go for a sail."

"Hurrah! Hurrah!" cried Donald and Goofy.

Donald was so pleased he made a little song. He went around all the evening singing it. He sang:

"Tomorrow we'll sail across the sea —
Mickey and Goofy, the anchors, and me.
And, oh, what fun, what fun it will be!"

The next morning Goofy came down to the shore very early. He looked the boat over carefully to be sure it was all right. And, oh dear, what do you think he found?

He found a hole in the front part of the boat. There had been a knot in one of the boards. The knot must have fallen out. Goofy looked for it, but he could not find it in the sand.

"Oh! Oh!" said Goofy. "Now, if we start, the water will come right in at the front of the boat. It will fill the boat. Poor Mickey and Donald will be *so* disappointed!"

Then he thought. "Why," said Goofy to himself, "I'll make a hole in the back part of the boat. Then, the water that comes in at the front will go out at the back. That's the best thing to do."

You can see that Goofy wasn't much of a sailor.

He hurried away for a drill and made a hole in the back of the boat. He liked to drill holes, so he made six or seven.

"Now the water can run right out," he said.

Mickey and Donald were coming. So Goofy hid the drill behind a rock.

"I won't tell them about the holes," said Goofy. "There's no use worrying them, now that everything's fixed."

Donald had brought a big box of lunch. Mickey had brought a pair of bellows. He thought the bellows would be useful if the wind died down.

They put the anchors into the boat and dragged it down into the water. They all got in, and Donald set the sail.

A puff of wind took them a little way out into the lake.

"Oh, look!" said Mickey, "water is coming into the boat!"

"It'll go out again," said Goofy.

But it didn't. In a very few minutes the boat sank. It went right to the bottom of the lake.

They were still quite near the shore. Mickey and Goofy found themselves up to their necks in water. The top of the mast was out of the water. Donald climbed up on this.

"Say, fellows," he cried. "We didn't make a boat. We made a submarine."

"It's queer," said Mickey. "There weren't any holes in the boat yesterday."

37

"We'd better go home," said Goofy. So they all swam ashore, and then went home for dry clothes.

Goofy decided to come back later and get the drill. He didn't say anything to Mickey or Donald about it. He thought it wasn't the right time to speak of all those holes. Some other day would be better.

THE FIRE ENGINE

One day Mickey and Donald played they were firemen. They played a long time. Goofy came and played with them.

"I'd like to be a real fireman," said Mickey.

"I'm going to be a real fireman," said Donald.

"So am I," said Goofy.

At last Goofy said he was hungry and went home. Donald went home with Goofy. Mickey sat down under a tree to rest.

Suddenly he heard a cry, "Fire! Fire! Fire!"

He looked down the road. Flames were coming out of the Disneyville Hotel. People were running out of the doors and climbing out of the windows.

"Oh! Oh! Something will have to be done," cried Mickey.

Just then he saw the Disneyville fire engine. It was standing beside the road not far away. No one was running it. There were no firemen. Just the engine and hose were there. Some firemen's hats were on the seat of the engine.

Mickey shouted, "Donald! Goofy!" as loud as he could.

Donald and Goofy came running.

"The hotel is burning. We'll have
to put out the fire!" cried Mickey.

"The firemen must have gone to a picnic, or something, and left the engine here. Jump on behind and get the hose ready. I'll drive."

Mickey got on the front seat and started the fire engine down the road. Donald and Goofy climbed in behind all ready to unwind the hose. The three put on firemen's hats.

The engine flew down the road with its bell ringing. It was a grand sight. Some people on the street stopped and stared. Others ran after the fire engine.

When they came to the burning hotel, Mickey and his friends quickly got the hose ready. Mickey took hold of the hose, and Donald turned on the water.

The hose was big and there was a
great deal of water. When the water
came through, the hose swung Mickey
right around. But the others helped
him, and they were able to play some
water on the fire.

Donald dashed into the house. He wanted to save some one. He thought it would be fine to be a hero.

He saw a hat-rack with a coat and hat on it. He thought the hat-rack was a girl. So he grabbed it and dragged it out.

"Don't be afraid," he said to the hat-rack. "I will save you."

Goofy took a red ax from the fire engine. He went up a tree and onto the roof. Then he began chopping holes.

This didn't do the roof any good, but Goofy thought it was the right thing to do. He had once seen a fireman chop a hole in a roof. So he was sure that chopping holes was part of putting out a fire.

By this time Mickey had the hose
turned on the roof. He did not
see Goofy. The stream of water
washed Goofy and his ax right off the
roof.

The hotel garden had just been
ploughed and raked. Goofy fell into
the soft earth and wasn't hurt at all.
He was well covered with dirt, but
he didn't mind that.

Before long, the fire was out. Then Mickey and Donald and Goofy rode away on the fire engine.

All the people cheered them.

The bell on the engine rang and rang. The people said, "Hurrah for Mickey! Hurrah for Donald! Hurrah for Goofy!"

Mickey took the fire engine back to the place where he had found it.

Just as he got there, all the real firemen came hurrying up the road. They had been to the woods for a picnic, and they looked very jolly. They were carrying picnic baskets and bunches of flowers.

When they saw Donald and Mickey and Goofy on the fire engine, they were very angry.

"Get down off that engine at once, you young rascals," roared the fire chief.

"Let me explain, Mr. Fire Chief," said Mickey politely.

"Don't talk to me! Get down!" cried the angry fire chief.

"I'll explain," shouted Donald, losing his temper. "The Disneyville Hotel would have burned down if it hadn't been for us. While you were having a picnic, Mickey and Goofy and I were putting out the fire. Go and look at the hotel. Ask anybody. Ask *anybody!*"

The firemen soon found that what Donald had told them was true. They thanked Mickey and Donald and Goofy, again and again.

The fire chief parked the fire engine beside the road. He took Donald and Mickey and Goofy and all the firemen to the drug store, and they had all the ice cream cones they could eat.

The drug store man made a new kind of ice cream soda just for them. He called it a "Fireman's Special." They each had one of those, too.

It was a great day.

DONALD THE WOODCUTTER

Some men had been working near
Donald Duck's house. One of the
men left his ax near a tree. He was
coming back later to cut the tree
down. It was an old tree and of no
real use.

Donald came along and picked up
the ax. He had never cut down a
tree, but he thought it would be fun
to try.

Just then Monty Mouse and Morty Mouse came along. They were nephews of Mickey and Minnie. They were orphans and often came to visit.

"Oh, oh, Donald," said Monty and Morty, "can you cut down a great big tree like that?"

"Yes, indeed," said Donald. "This isn't much of a tree. Watch me bring it down. Stand back so the chips won't hit you."

"Oh, my!" said Monty.

"Oh, my!" said Morty.

Now, Donald liked to boast about what he could do. He was clever, and he could do a great many things well, but sometimes he boasted too soon. This was one of those times.

Up in the tree hung a big gray nest. It was a wasps' nest. The reason the workman had not cut down the tree was because he was afraid of the wasps.

Donald was not afraid. He didn't know a wasps' nest when he saw one.

He stood away from the tree. Then he swung the ax hard and hit the tree a terrible blow. The tree shook, and the wasps' nest shook, too.

Donald swung the ax again, and again the wasps' nest was badly shaken.

He swung the ax a third time. Crash went the ax into the tree — and down came the wasps' nest at Donald's feet. The wasps were already flying out of it.

Monty and Morty had seen the wasps when the nest began to fall. They ran away as fast as they could. You wouldn't have believed short legs could get over the ground as fast as theirs did.

Donald ran, too, but he had stopped a moment to see what it was that fell. The wasps came out of the nest in a swarm. They all followed him as he ran.

How he ran! He fairly flew down the road, with the cloud of wasps all around him — then out on the little boat dock at the lake.

The wasps had begun to sting. So Donald didn't wait a minute. He jumped into the lake. It was the only way to escape.

The wasps left when Donald went into the lake. But the lake was very low. Donald found himself in more mud than water. He tried to get ashore, and found that he was stuck in the mud.

He called and called. Monty and
Morty heard him and came running.
When they saw what had happened
to Donald, they ran back and got a
stout fish pole.

They wound the line around the pole and tied it so that the fish-hook was close to the pole. Then they reached down with the pole. They caught the hook in Donald's blouse. Working hard, they pulled him up until he could reach the dock.

Poor Donald was a sad sight. He was covered with mud from his head to his feet.

Morty helped Donald brush off the mud and water. Monty ran back and got his cap. It had come off when he was running away from the wasps.

"Thank you very much, Monty and Morty," said Donald. "Of course I could have got out by myself. But it would have taken me quite a while."

"Oh, that's all right, Donald," said
Monty and Morty. "We were glad

to help you. You are the biggest fish
we ever caught. Now, will you let us
see you cut the tree down?"

"No," said Donald. "I need a rest. I don't think I'll cut down any more trees today."

"But you haven't cut down any trees," said Morty.

"You cut down wasps," said Monty.

"And the wasps cut up," said Morty.

"Ha, ha, ha!" said Monty.

"Ha, ha, ha!" said Morty.

They ran off toward home, laughing hard.

"I don't see anything to laugh at," said Donald crossly. Then he started for home, too.

As he walked along, he said, "They ought to be spanked." That was all he said. Perhaps he meant the wasps, and perhaps he meant Monty and Morty.

DONALD THE EXPLORER

It was snowing. Donald Duck was indoors reading. His book was about an explorer who had been to the South Pole.

There were three or four pictures of penguins in the book. Donald liked to look at these pictures.

"I'd like to see some penguins," said Donald to himself. "This book says they are very hard to catch.

"The explorer didn't bring any back with him. He had some, but they got away. When I go to the South Pole, I shall bring back a lot of penguins. They won't get away from me."

He turned the page and went on reading. The more he read, the more he wanted to go to the South Pole.

By and by, he looked out of the window. He was surprised to see Goofy coming slowly through the deep snow.

Goofy was walking on skis. He was dragging a sled. The sled was piled high with all kinds of bundles and packages.

Donald pulled on his sweater. He grabbed his muffler and cap. Then he ran out to meet Goofy.

"Hi, Goof," he said, "where are you going with all that stuff?"

"I'm going to the South Pole," said Goofy. "I hear it's a fine trip. I have blankets and food and other things on my sled."

"Will you let me go, too?" asked Donald.

"Yes," said Goofy, "if you'll help pull the sled."

"I will," said Donald. "Just wait till I get some things. I can put them on your sled."

He ran quickly into the house. In a short time he came back carrying a butterfly net, a large bird cage, and a package. He put these on Goofy's sled with the other things.

"What are you going to do with those things, Donald?" asked Goofy.

"I shall catch some young penguins with the net," said Donald, "and I'll bring them back in the cage."

"What's in the package?" asked Goofy.

"A black coat and a white shirt," said Donald. "I'm going to wear them.

That ought to fool the penguins.
They'll think I'm another penguin
when they see me all black and
white."

"They say penguins are pretty
smart," said Goofy.

"Well, even if they are, I'm going
to catch one," said Donald. "They
aren't any smarter than I am."

They started out. Goofy pulled the
sled and Donald pushed.

Perhaps you think it took them a
long time to reach the South Pole.

But they went very fast and got there very quickly.

They made a hole in the ice and caught some fish. They put these away to cook for supper.

"We'd better make a snow house," said Goofy.

"You start the house. I'm going to catch a penguin right away," said Donald.

Goofy helped Donald dress himself in the black coat and white shirt.

When he was dressed, he really did look a little like a penguin.

Then Donald tied a fish to a short pole by a string. This was bait for catching penguins. He also carried with him the butterfly net and the bird cage.

Donald walked along for some time. At last he saw something small and black in the snow. He set down the bird cage and walked toward the little black thing.

Sure enough, he had found a baby penguin.

The baby did not run away. It stood and stared at Donald.

Donald held out the stick he carried, so that the fish hung right in front of the little penguin's bill.

But the penguin suddenly grew frightened. It turned and began to hurry away. Donald followed. He tried to get the butterfly net over the baby penguin's head. But the little penguin was too quick. It hurried off crying, "Oo-lah! Oo-lah! Oo-lah!"

In no time at all penguins rushed in from all sides — big penguins, little penguins, and middle-sized penguins. It seemed to Donald that there must have been a penguin hiding behind every snow-bank.

Two of the biggest penguins took hold of Donald, one on each side, as though they were policemen.

Donald tried to tell them that he did not mean to hurt the little penguin. But the penguins could not understand him, and he could not understand them. He was sure of only one thing. This was that the penguins were angry at him.

As the penguins stood holding Donald, the biggest penguin of all came up.

What do you suppose he was carrying? Donald's bird cage.

One of the penguins opened the door of the cage. The two policemen penguins pushed Donald in and shut the door.

Donald was badly frightened. "How can I ever get out?" he thought.

The penguins all walked around the cage and made fun of him. He was sure they were laughing at him, though everything they said sounded like "Oo-lah!"

After a while they stopped laughing and joking. They all gathered in a huddle and talked together. Donald felt that they were planning what to do with him. He grew more and more worried.

Suddenly he thought of Goofy. Perhaps Goofy could scare away the penguins. He began to shout and pound on the cage. He hoped Goofy would hear him.

But Goofy did not come and Donald at last stopped shouting. It was no use. He was sure of that.

The penguins came out of their
huddle and went to a snow hill a little
way off. There they began coasting.
They sat on flat pieces of ice and slid
down hill on these. They seemed to
be having a great deal of fun.

Donald knew he could open the
cage door if he had a chance. He
hoped that the penguins would stop
watching him.

When they seemed very busy coasting, he unfastened the door. He unfastened it, but left it closed. He would push it open when he had a chance.

One penguin on his ice sled ran into another penguin on his. There was quite a mix-up. The penguins did not seem to be watching the cage.

Donald took off his black coat. He hung it on one side of the cage. Then he quickly dropped to the floor, pushed the door open, and crawled out.

He hoped the penguins would see the black coat and think he was still in the cage. He had on the white shirt. This would keep them from seeing him as he crawled along in the snow.

The penguins didn't see Donald. Or else they saw him and didn't mind. They had thought it was a good joke to scare him. But now they were busy coasting. They had lost interest in him. Penguins are like that.

Donald crawled a long way in the snow before he dared stand up and walk. At last he saw Goofy and the snow house. Goofy was out looking for him.

"Hurry, Donald! The fish have cooked till they are all dried up," called Goofy.

"I've had a terrible time, Goofy!" said Donald.

"That's too bad," said Goofy. "Come inside and tell me about it. Did you see any penguins?"

"Yes, I did," said Donald, "and I never want to see another penguin — never, *never*, NEVER! I don't like the South Pole, anyhow. You ought not to have brought me here."

"Well, we don't have to stay," said the good-natured Goofy. "We'll go back in the morning."

So they went back home the next day. That was the end of the famous Goofy–Donald Polar Expedition.

THE THREE LITTLE PIGS

Minnie Mouse was making apple pies. Morty Mouse and Monty Mouse were watching her. After she had made six big pies, Minnie made two little apple turnovers. One was for Monty and one was for Morty.

"Minnie," said Monty, "will you tell us a story while the turnovers are cooking?"

"You know all my stories," said Minnie.

"Well," said Morty, "can't you tell us another one about the Three Little Pigs?"

"Oh, yes," said Minnie. "I know one I haven't told you."

This is the story Minnie told:

Once upon a time there were three little pigs. One of them was a very practical, sensible fellow. The other two were very foolish and needed a great deal of watching.

One day the Practical Pig went to town to do some shopping.

Before he went he said, "Brothers, I want you to pull weeds in the garden while I am away. And will you pick up the apples under the big red apple tree?"

The two Foolish Pigs said, "Yes, Brother," very politely, and the Practical Pig started for town.

When he came back, he went to the garden. He was going to help his brothers.

But they were not there. The Practical Pig could not see them anywhere.

"Oh, dear! Oh, dear!" he said. "They have wandered off. I am afraid the Big Bad Wolf has caught them. I must think quickly what to do to save them."

The Big Bad Wolf had a house in a
mountain side a few miles away.   He
lived there with his three little sons.
They were all very fond of roast pork.

The Practical Pig knew this.   He
had often warned his brothers about
the Big Bad Wolf.

But the two Foolish Pigs always laughed at his warnings. They were not careful. Their favorite song was one named "Who's Afraid of the Big Bad Wolf?"

Soon after the Practical Pig went to town, his brothers grew tired of pulling weeds. So they left the garden and started walking along the road to the mountain. They liked that road because many berries grew along the way.

They were picking berries and singing, "Who's Afraid of the Big Bad Wolf?" when they saw a stranger coming. She wore a queer-looking dress and hat, and she carried a long crook in her hand. She seemed to be crying.

"How do you do, sirs?" said the
stranger. "I am Little Bo Peep. I
have lost my sheep. Will you help
me find them and drive them home?
You look so handsome and clever, I
am sure you can help me."

The two Foolish Pigs were pleased. No one had ever told them before that they were handsome and clever. (You can probably guess why.)

They walked on toward the mountain with Little Bo Peep. They watched carefully for her sheep, but they did not see even one lamb.

At last Bo Peep said, "You must be tired. Will you come into my house and rest? I shall have something very nice for dinner if you will stay." (This was quite true.)

So they went into a house in the mountain side with Bo Peep. As soon as they were inside, she slammed the door. Then she pulled off her big bonnet and her odd dress. Little Bo Peep was the Big Bad Wolf!

The three little wolves rushed forward to help their father. In a short time the two Foolish Pigs were tightly tied with strong cord. Then they were put in a big roasting pan with some large potatoes.

The oven was cold. So the Big Bad Wolf made a fire and waited for the oven to get hot before cooking his dinner. This was lucky for the little pigs.

The poor Foolish Pigs were very unhappy. To make matters worse the three little wolves marched round and round the table singing. They sang:

"Now we'll have some nice roast pig,
    Nice roast pig,
    Nice roast pig,
Now we'll have some nice roast pig,
    Tra, la, la, la, la!"

There came a ring at the doorbell. The Big Bad Wolf went to the door.

A peddler was there. He had a basket of big red apples.

"Do you want to buy some apples?" he asked. "I'm hungry; so I'll give you the whole basketful if you'll let me stay to dinner."

"Oh, all right," said the Wolf. "Come in."

The peddler was small, but he had a heavy wrench in one hand. So the Big Bad Wolf thought he had better not try to take the apples without paying for them.

You would not have guessed it, but the peddler was really the Practical Pig. He had on a wig and a big black mustache and false eyebrows.

Even his brothers didn't know him at first.

"Those apples will be good with our roast pork," said the Wolf.

"Aren't you going to make apple sauce?" asked the peddler.

"No. The sauce-pan is down in the cellar. I don't want to bother getting it," said the Wolf.

"Oh, all right, if you feel that way about it," said the peddler. "The best people *always* have apple sauce with their roast pork. But perhaps it's not important."

"I suppose we may as well have apple sauce. We usually have it," said the Wolf. This was not true, but he wanted the peddler to think he knew what was correct.

He unbolted a trap door, and climbed down a ladder into the cellar.

The peddler went to the trap door and looked over the edge.

"Is that a rat I see?" he asked.

"Where? Where? Where?" cried the three little wolves running to look, too.

"Down there," said the peddler; and he gave the three little wolves a push that sent them down into the cellar.

Then — quick as a flash — he slammed the trap door and bolted it. He pulled a table on top of the trap door and every other heavy thing he could find.

"Oh, the peddler is Brother," cried the frightened little pigs, joyfully.

The Practical Pig cut the cords that held his brothers, and they were soon out of the roasting pan. They were very much ashamed and very thankful.

At first the two Foolish Pigs were rather quiet on the way home. But, by and by, they began to sing. The Practical Pig joined in and they all sang together:

"Who's afraid of the Big Bad Wolf,
Big Bad Wolf,
Big Bad Wolf?
Who's afraid of the Big Bad Wolf?
Tra, la, la, la, la!"

Minnie stopped talking and hurried to the oven. The pies and turnovers were done. They smelled fine.

"Minnie," said Monty, "did the wolves ever get out of the cellar?"

"Oh, yes," said Minnie, "they got out. But it took them four or five hours."

DONALD'S LUCKY DAY

Mickey Mouse was watering the flowers in his yard. Pluto was with him. They looked up and saw Donald Duck coming on his new bicycle. Donald was wearing a blue suit trimmed with red, and he had on a blue cap trimmed with red.

"Hello, Donald," said Mickey. "You look fine. Where did you get that outfit?"

"It's my uniform. I'm a messenger boy," said Donald proudly. "I take messages and packages to all parts of town. It's very important work. It takes a person with brains to do it."

"How long have you been doing it?" asked Pluto.

"I began this afternoon," said Donald.

"You didn't pick a very good day to begin," said Pluto. "This is Friday the thirteenth. Friday's an unlucky day and thirteen is an unlucky number."

"Oh, Pluto, you don't believe that stuff, do you?" said Mickey.

"Well, Goofy told me Friday is unlucky," said Pluto. "And he says thirteen is unlucky. He says it's unlucky to go under a ladder, it's unlucky if you break a mirror, and it's very unlucky if a black cat goes across your path."

"I don't know about all that," said Mickey, "but it'll be unlucky for my flowers if I don't water them. If Donald has a message to carry, it'll be unlucky for him if he doesn't go ahead with it."

"Oh, my goodness!" said Donald, "I have to go and get a box from a man. I almost forgot about it. I'm not worried about today being Friday the thirteenth, though. This is my lucky day."

He rode away on his bicycle, singing a song he had heard on the radio.

"No matter what you say
Good luck will come my way
I'll have no fears,
I'll shed no tears,
This is my lucky day."

He was so busy riding and singing that he almost ran down a man who was selling toy mice. They were the kind of mice that run when they are wound up.

The man was angry at Donald. He said he would call a policeman. So Donald bought a toy mouse to make him feel better. Then he rode on.

At last he reached the house he had been sent to. He rang the bell and a man came to the door. He gave Donald a box. "Take this box to the address that is written on it," said the man, "and don't waste any time."

Donald put the box into the carrier on his handle bars. Then he rode off, singing loudly, "This is my lucky day."

When he had gone a little way, he looked at the address on the box.

Miss Ima Jinks,
1313 West 13th Street.

"Oh, boy!" said Donald. "I suppose Goofy would say this box would bring me bad luck. I'd better be careful."

He slowed up very suddenly and almost fell off his bicycle. For right in front of him was a long ladder.

It reached from the sidewalk to the
wall of a house. Donald had nearly
gone under it.

"Ha, ha!" said Donald to the ladder.
"I fooled you that time." He started
to cross the street. "I'll ride on the
other side," he thought. "I don't
believe in this bad luck stuff, but
I may as well be careful."

Across the street was a second-hand furniture store. A good many pieces of furniture were on the sidewalk in front of it.

When Donald was nearly across, an automobile dashed around the corner. Donald hurried ahead to get out of the way of the automobile and bounced up on the sidewalk.

Before he could stop, his front wheel hit a mirror. It was quite a big mirror. The wheel struck it hard and smashed it into bits.

Donald wasn't hurt. He hurried off as fast as his bicycle would take him.

"It may be bad luck to break a mirror. But I think I was pretty lucky not to get cut on all that glass," said Donald.

He didn't stop to think about the bad luck of the poor man who owned the mirror.

He rode on until he came to a place where men were digging. A large new building was to be put up.

Donald was a little tired. He got off .his bicycle and sat down on a stone to watch the workers. He put the box on the grass near by.

Donald spoke to one of the men. "There are lots of big rocks in this place," he said. "How are you going to get them out?"

"We'll blast the biggest ones out with giant powder," said the man. "We're going to blow up one today."

Donald walked around a little to see what was being done.

Then he picked up his box, put it in the carrier, and started on again. He did not notice that he had picked up the wrong box. The one for Miss Ima Jinks was still lying on the grass where he had left it. The box he had picked up had giant powder in it. It held enough powder to blow up a big rock.

Donald rode along and came at last
to the corner of Thirteenth Avenue
and Thirteenth Street.

He was just turning the corner
when a black cat started across the
sidewalk in front of him.

Donald began to feel a little frightened. All the things Pluto had spoken about seemed to be happening to him. "Scat!" he cried. "Go away, cat! Go away!"

He kept turning his bicycle to keep the cat from going in front of him. The cat seemed to want to pass in front of him and nowhere else.

Donald suddenly remembered the toy mouse. He got off his bicycle. The cat sat down a little way off and looked at him.

Donald took the mouse out of his pocket and wound it. Then he put it down. It started quickly and went whirring around the corner. The cat dashed after it. "Well, that's over," said Donald.

Thirteenth Street was very short. Donald knew he must be near the house that was numbered 1313. So he picked up the box, and left his bicycle where it was.

But the toy mouse had changed its direction, as toy mice do. In a moment it went whirring past him. Donald looked back and saw the black cat coming.

He made up his mind not to let the cat pass in front of him. There was a dock at the end of the street. He ran out on the dock, carrying the box, and sat down on a log.

The toy mouse ran out on the dock, too. It reached the edge and fell off into the water. The cat followed the mouse, but not into the water.

Donald jumped up. As he did so, he noticed the label on top of the box. It did not say "Miss Ima Jinks." It said, "Danger. Giant Powder."

In his fright, Donald caught his toe on a board. The box shot out of his hands into the water.

It must have struck a rock or an anchor.

Bang! There was an awful crash.

All the water in the lake seemed to come up over the dock. Donald was washed off the dock and then back on it again.

When the water rolled away, it left a big pile of fish. They had been killed by the blast from the giant powder. Donald found himself sitting in the middle of the pile.

Soon he saw the black cat. She was very wet, but she came hurrying to the pile of fish with a cheerful face.

In a short time she was followed by all her friends and relatives. Dozens of cats lived about the docks. They all smelled the fish and came to the party in a hurry — thin cats, fat cats, big cats, little cats and middle-sized cats.

And how they ate! The pile of fish became fish-bones very rapidly.

"Well, kits," said Donald, "this is your lucky day. It's mine, too. I might have been blown to bits. Black cats don't bring *me* bad luck."

He walked back, dripping, to his bicycle. As he walked, he sang,

"I'll have no fears,
I'll shed no tears,
This is my lucky day."